MERMAIDS on PARADE

Melanie Hope Greenberg

Melanie Hope Greenberg

G. P. Putnam's Sons

Once a year when vacation starts I march in a parade to celebrate the opening of the ocean during the summer solstice.

This year I will march in the parade as a
"Shy Mermaid Coming Out of Her Shell."

Mom, Dad and I get ready. Mom helps me into my jeweled costume, while Dad glues starfish to my seashell wagon.

ASTROLAND
CYCLONE
FUN
WIN
WIN
FUN
WIN
GIFT SHOP
FUN

Marchers arrive early and crowd into
my Coney Island neighborhood.
The ocean air smells extra salty.
The streets are electric with excitement.

FRUITS AND VEGETABLES
EAST RIVER
MERMAIDS

Today is the day when mermaids,
Neptunes and other legendary sea creatures
leave their oceans to walk on land.

WONDER WHEEL
ASTROLAND
EAT
SEA FOOD
CONEY ISLAND
HOT DOGS
SHAKES
RIDES
CONES
FUN
FRIES
EARTH FIRST
MERMAIDS on PARADE

We line up. Shiny costumes sparkle and glitter.
Marchers are each given a badge. Mine says number 55.
King Neptune and Queen Mermaid lead the parade
of gorgeous glistening creatures.
The heat rising from the steamy sidewalk
makes them seem to sway and shimmer.
I can hear ocean waves pounding onto the shore
and my heart beats faster.

There are rows and rows of
onlookers along the boardwalk.

Clap! Clap! Clap! They cheer and applaud,
then click their cameras. Snap! Snap! Snap!

In front of us are Brooklyn's East River Mermaids.
They bring their own music.
I get chills down my spine each time
they spin and twirl and dance and whirl.

Now the parade makes a turn
to march along Surf Avenue.

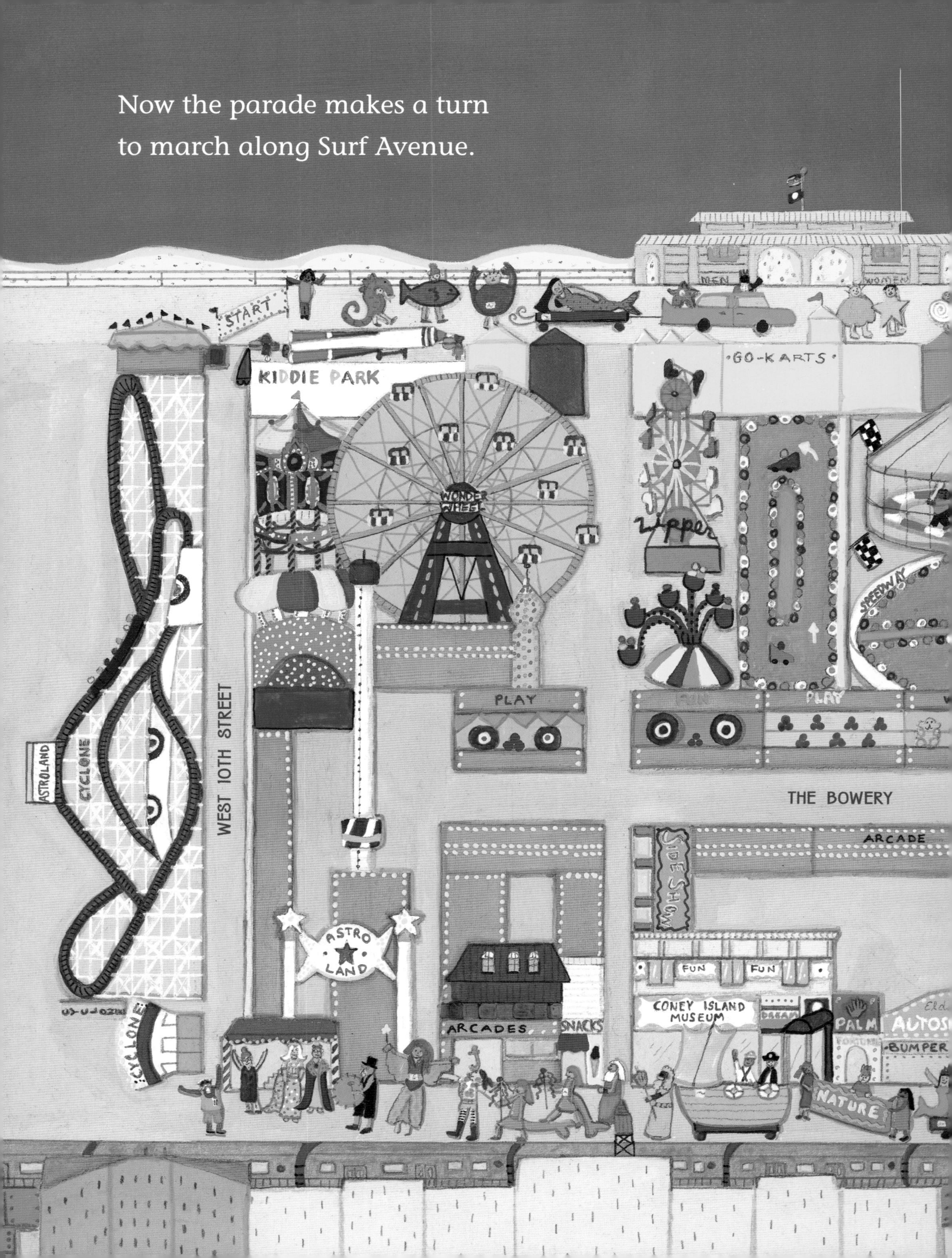

Screechy brakes from the subway trains overhead set off tiny fireworks, shooting sparks of light to join in the celebration.

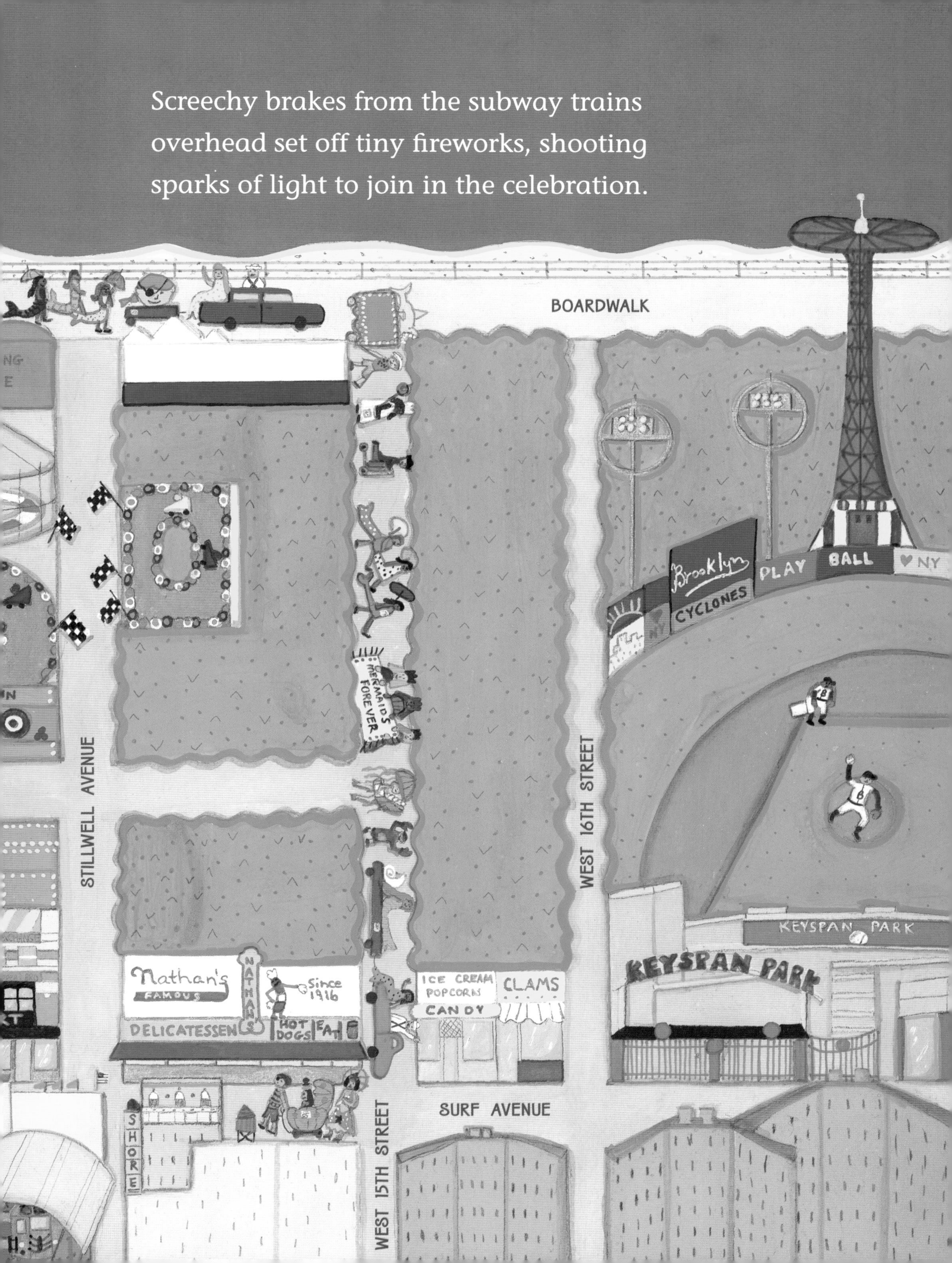

BMT
STILLWELL
BMT
POLICE
POLICE
50
51
52
55
48
53
LIL NEPTUNE
47
49

The sun feels warm and tingly on my skin
as we wait for floats and performers
to stop in front of the judges' stand.
The music and cheering are so loud.
What are the judges saying?
Who will win the trophies?

A moving stream of marchers and onlookers follow the King and Queen down the beach to the water.

Queen Mermaid cuts four ribbons along the way.
Snip! Snip! Snip! Autumn, winter, spring.
Then a Snip! for summer and the ocean is open to all.

The King and Queen toss juicy fruits into
the salty sea for a good summer of swimming.
Mangoes, pineapples and bananas bob up and down

before they sink below to feed the sea gods and goddesses. Sea foam tickles my toes.

After the parade is over, everyone spreads out to play
and thrill on amusement park rides and attractions.
Or they meet on the boardwalk for food and cool drinks.

But Mom, Dad and I can't wait
to go back to the judges' stand.

BEST
MUSIC
GROUP
55

We look at trophies that say Best Music Group,
Best Neptune and Best Mermaid.
Then I see a trophy with number 55 on it.
That's my number! I won a trophy!
Waves of joy lift me higher and higher.
I am voted Best Little Mermaid!

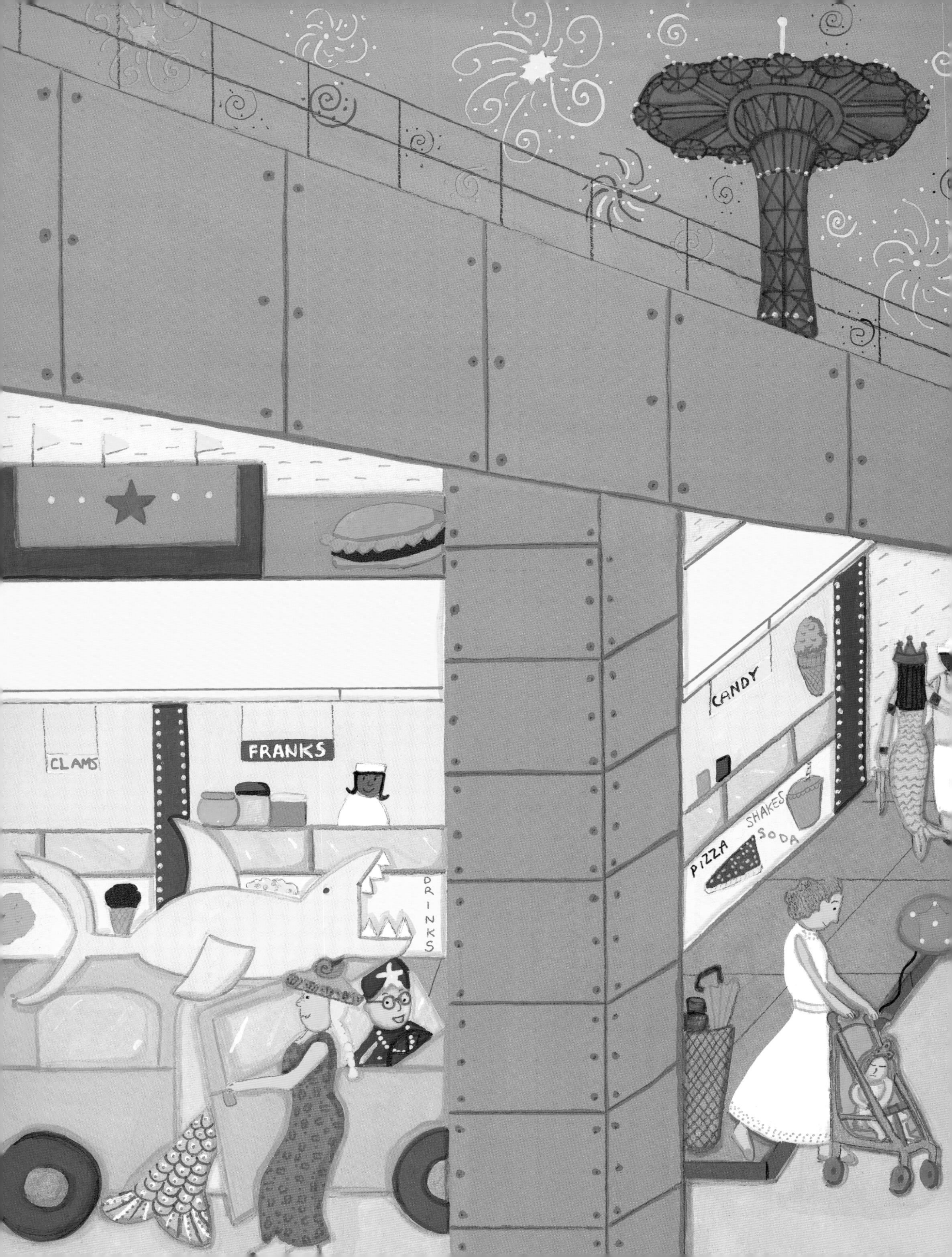
CLAMS
FRANKS
DRINKS
CANDY
SHAKES
SODA
PIZZA

I marched with mermaids, Neptunes and
sea creatures today.
Tomorrow, the magical creatures will all be gone.
Whether they return to the sea or just return
to their neighborhoods until next year,
I have my trophy to remember them always.

HOW TO MAKE A MERMAID TAIL IN 3 EASY STEPS

YOU WILL NEED:

- Fabric or craft paper
- Pencil
- Scissors

YOU MIGHT ALSO WISH TO USE:

- Glue, crayons, markers, seashells, pipe cleaners, pom-poms, sequins, buttons, feathers, glitter, starfish, and more.

Be sure that the fabric/craft paper is wide enough to tie around your waist.

Make sure the length of your tail goes from your waist to the floor.

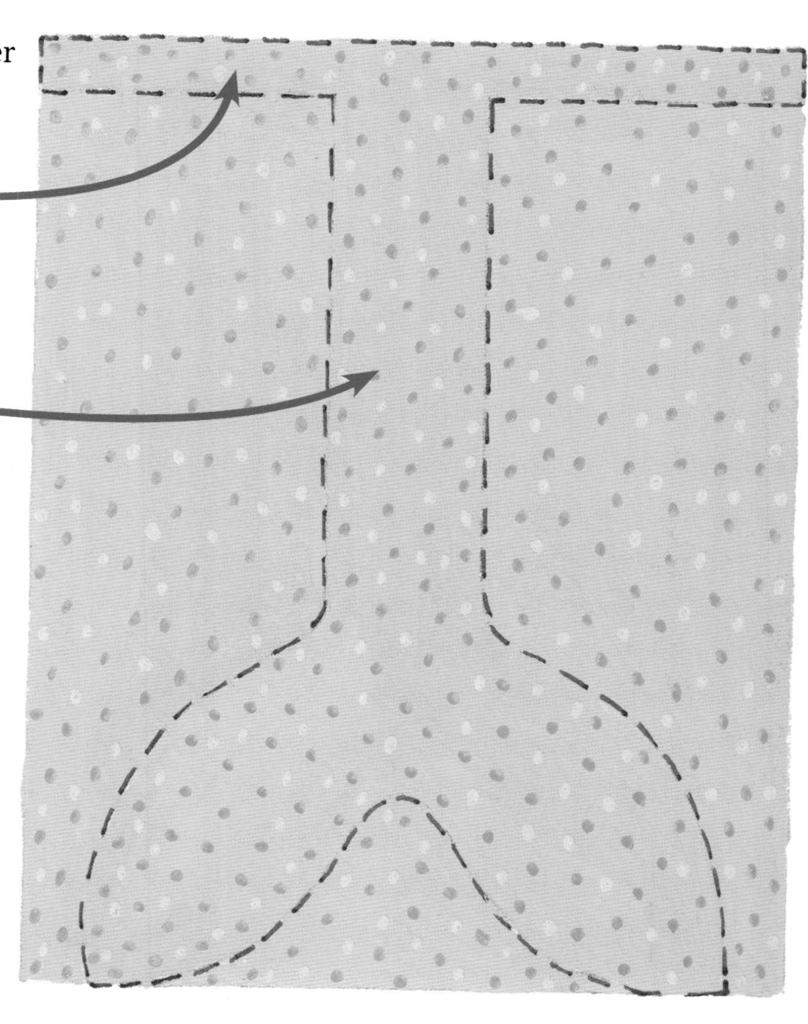

1) DRAW the shape of the tail.

2) CUT along the shape.

3) DECORATE!

AUTHOR'S NOTE

Beginning in the 1870s, Coney Island, Brooklyn, was a well-known vacation playground. Besides its beckoning beaches, it was world famous for its amusement parks, particularly Steeplechase, Luna Park and Dreamland, where one could taste the future through the wonders of machines.

Dreamland's manager, Samuel Gompertz, founded a carnival-style parade he called the Mardi Gras in 1903. Mardi Gras was the culmination of a weeklong celebration ending the summer beach season. Early parade floats glided along Surf Avenue attached to overhead trolley lines, illuminated by the newly modern use of electricity. Sadly, the Mardi Gras ended in 1954.

In 1983, an updated Mardi Gras called the Mermaid Parade rekindled a spark of Coney Island's unique heritage and colorful mythology. The parade is now held at the beginning of the beach season as a summer solstice ritual to open the ocean. The parade stars hundreds of New York City's creative and talented artists, musicians and performers, as well as everyday folk who transform into zestful dazzling mermaids, pirates, Neptunes and sea creatures. Thousands of spectators gather together to cheer on the fun, the fantasy and the child spirit in everyone.

For Deloris McCullough, David Mowery, Tanya Rynd, Superfine, Tim Travaglini and Cecilia Yung.

Special thanks to those who march within these pages: Sabine Arorowsky, Jay Asher, Pasqualina Azzarello, Stella Barnstool, Alex Battles, Jan Bell, Juliette Campbell, Bill Carney, Josh Coleman, Eve Collins, Cary Curran, Joseph Dejarnette, Steve DeSeve, Helene Deme Elzevir, Lisa Flores, Tanya Gagne, Tim Galbreath, Sue Ganz-Shmitt, Tim Gerken, Anna Goodman, Amy Gordon, Petra Hanson, Eri Hanyu, Aubrey Heimer, Herb Hernandez, India Holiday, Virpi Kanervo, Shannon Kerner, Melissa Koehler, Alex Krivosheiw, Yung and Simone LePage, Cat Mantione, Robin Mellom, Ben and Jasmine Moran, Keith Moss, Brian Mulroney, Veronica Otto, Paranoid Larry, Eve Porinchak, Evan Reynolds, Page Rockwell, Leif Rodriequez, Lila and Robbie Rynd, Sanford Santacroce, Gil Schuster, Laura Sewell, Amber Shon, Gavin Smith, Julie Sommerville, Cara Lee Sparry, Laura Taylor, Jaimie Walker, Anastasia Woodworth, Dedre and Drake Wright, Julia Zaychenko, and Julianne Zeleta.

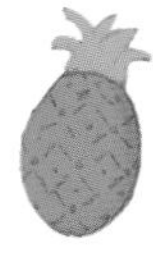

G. P. PUTNAM'S SONS
A division of Penguin Young Readers Group.
Published by The Penguin Group.
Penguin Group (USA) Inc., 375 Hudson Street, New York, NY 10014, U.S.A.
Penguin Group (Canada), 90 Eglinton Avenue East, Suite 700, Toronto, Ontario M4P 2Y3, Canada (a division of Pearson Penguin Canada Inc.).
Penguin Books Ltd, 80 Strand, London WC2R 0RL, England.
Penguin Ireland, 25 St. Stephen's Green, Dublin 2, Ireland (a division of Penguin Books Ltd.).
Penguin Group (Australia), 250 Camberwell Road, Camberwell, Victoria 3124, Australia (a division of Pearson Australia Group Pty Ltd).
Penguin Books India Pvt Ltd, 11 Community Centre, Panchsheel Park, New Delhi - 110 017, India.
Penguin Group (NZ), 67 Apollo Drive, Rosedale, North Shore 0632, New Zealand (a division of Pearson New Zealand Ltd).
Penguin Books (South Africa) (Pty) Ltd, 24 Sturdee Avenue, Rosebank, Johannesburg 2196, South Africa.
Penguin Books Ltd, Registered Offices: 80 Strand, London WC2R 0RL, England.

Manufactured in China by South China Printing Co. Ltd.
Design by Richard Amari.
Text set in ITC Stone Informal.
The artist used gouache, pen and pencil on 140-pound cold press watercolor paper to create the illustrations for this book.
Library of Congress Cataloging-in-Publication Data
Greenberg, Melanie Hope. Mermaids on parade / Melanie Hope Greenberg. p. cm. Summary: A young girl participates in Coney Island's Mermaid Parade to celebrate the opening of the ocean during the summer solstice. [1. Parades—Fiction. 2. Summer—Fiction. 3. Beaches—Fiction. 4. Coney Island (New York, N.Y.)—Fiction.] I. Title.
PZ7.G82755Mer 2008 [E]—dc22 2007016586
ISBN 978-0-399-24708-8
1 3 5 7 9 10 8 6 4 2

http://mermaidsonparade.blogspot.com
www.melaniehopegreenberg.com
Join my EMAIL LIST:
melanie@melaniehopegreenberg.com